First Catch Your Gran

Lizzie was a girl who usually got what she wanted. And not by whining, screaming or throwing a tantrum. Perhaps she was just more realistic than most nine year olds. After all, if you cry for the moon you are usually left moonless and still crying. When Lizzie wanted something, she *made* it happen, instead of hanging around vaguely hoping that somebody else would do it for her. And that's why all this began.

One Saturday afternoon she came into the kitchen and said, "Mum, where's my gran?"

Her mother looked surprised, but went on ironing.

"She died, Lizzie, you know she did. When you were only ten months old. We've been through all this before. It was sad, but she was old and very ill."

"Well, what about my other one, then? Lucy's got two grannies."

"You mean your dad's mother? She died too, even longer ago. I never even knew her."

"So there are no grannies. And no grandpas left, either?"

CONTENTS

Lizzie's List

Maggie Harrison
Illustrations by Bethan Matthews

WALKER BOOKS
AND SUBSIDIARIES
LONDON • BOSTON • SYDNEY

To adoptions in general
and to Tabitha, Charity
and John in particular,
because they will know why.

First published 1991 by Walker Books Ltd
87 Vauxhall Walk, London SE11 5HJ

This edition published 1997

2 4 6 8 10 9 7 5 3

Text © 1991 Maggie Harrison
Illustrations © 1991 Bethan Matthews
Cover illustration © 1997 Bethan Matthews

This book has been typeset in Sabon.

Printed and bound in Great Britain by
The Guernsey Press Co. Ltd

British Library Cataloguing in Publication Data
A catalogue record for this book is
available from the British Library.

ISBN 0-7445-5276-1

J110, 251   £3.99

CR

Books by the same author

Angels on Roller-skates

"Sorry love, it's a shame, because it's nice to have grandparents."

"Lucy goes to stay with hers and they spoil her. She likes it. They have a house near the sea, one lot does, and *her* granny…"

"Well, I'm sorry we didn't manage things better for you, Lizzie, but nobody lasts for ever, and there's nothing to be done about it. Your friend Lucy talks too much!"

Mum smoothed the cotton dungarees on the ironing board, then she smiled.

"I'm sorry there aren't any Granny shops, or I'd save up and buy one for you!"

"Don't be silly, Mum," Lizzie said, and wandered away. She trailed down seven flights of concrete stairs, thinking, and crossed over to the grassy play-area between the tall blocks of flats. She sat on a swing, still thinking, and rubbed a deep groove in the hard-packed earth with the edge of her trainers. Then she trailed all the way back to the flat.

"And there aren't any uncles or aunties are

there? Or cousins or anything? Just me and you."

"That's right, Lizzie, just you and me."

Lizzie went to her room, closed the door, found a felt-tip pen that still worked and made a list.

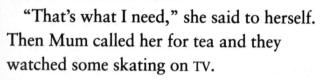

"That's what I need," she said to herself. Then Mum called her for tea and they watched some skating on TV.

The following Saturday Lizzie wandered round the shopping precinct watching all the elderly ladies. She had decided to find a granny for herself, but she wasn't at all sure how to choose one. She wished that she could have seen Lucy's grannies first, to give her some idea of what to look for.

There were a lot of older women shopping that morning, but none of them seemed quite right. Lizzie sighed. It was more difficult than she'd expected. The ones with well-cut hair, bounding along with loud jolly laughs and expensive, sensible shoes, looked like hard work. But the ones who pushed shopping trolleys, stopping to blink at all the crowds, weren't quite right either.

Lizzie sat down on one of the precinct's concrete benches, feeling discouraged. She had to admit that she knew absolutely nothing about real grannies, or even what made a good one. Why hadn't she asked Mum what her own gran had been like? Rather dark photographs in an old album showed her holding Lizzie as a baby. Now Lizzie felt a little ashamed to remember that she had always been more interested in looking at the baby than at the person holding her. She wasn't even sure what she wanted a granny to do. Other than belong to her, of course. And to stop her being so jealous of Lucy. Somebody she could visit, perhaps, and who could come to school with her mum to see the end of year play or to sports day. Perhaps she ought to ask Lucy to bring some photographs to school…

Lizzie was so busy trying to imagine what Lucy's grannies looked like, that she hardly noticed the elderly woman walking towards her bench. But when the woman sat down Lizzie glanced at her automatically. This one was definitely too severe. More like a retired headmistress than a granny, with that narrow, bony head and those sharp eyes. And she was scruffy. The corners of her duffle coat pockets needed sewing up. Proper grannies always mended clothes, and said things like "a stitch in time saves nine".
She wasn't even sure
that grannies

were supposed to wear duffle coats anyway, or dark red corduroy trousers. It didn't seem quite suitable somehow. And her hair was too short to stay tidy in this wind. Lizzie glanced furtively at her again. Yes, it was sticking up all over the place in grey and white tufts. Lucy's grannies probably had wavy white hair, neatly pinned into a respectable bun at the back. And they'd probably have been able to sit on their hair when they were young. People did in the old days. You often read that in books.

So far Lizzie hadn't talked to any of the old ladies she had seen, and none of them had talked to her – except for the ratty one

outside Debenham's who had been looking at her own reflection in the window, and who had told her she was a rude little girl for staring. Lizzie, partly because she was feeling so disappointed, decided that she might as well practise on this one. She looked the right age but the wrong sort. With longer hair she'd make a good witch, though, or second cousin to a witch anyway...

"I'm Lizzie Giles," Lizzie began bravely. "Who are you?"

"Mildred Peabody, Mrs."

"Oh," said Lizzie, and stopped. What could she say about "Mildred Peabody"? She could hardly say "that's a nice name", because she didn't think it was.

"I'm sorry," she said instead. And then wished she hadn't.

"I'm not," the woman replied pleasantly.

There was a pause.

"Where do you live? I live up there, on the seventh floor." Lizzie pointed to the nearest tower block.

"You must get a marvellous view from your balcony. I live in Barrow Lane, in one of those little terraced houses backing on to the canal."

Lizzie thought how lucky Lucy was, having a granny who lived near the sea, but all she said was, "Sounds good. To have a whole house of your own, and go upstairs to bed like in books. We've only ever lived in flats."

"Mm. I'll remember that next time my knees complain about going upstairs."

They both laughed, and Lizzie felt more comfortable. This lady wasn't as severe as she looked. After about twenty minutes of lively chatter, Lizzie decided Mildred Peabody, Mrs, wasn't exactly her idea of a granny but she might just do.

"Have you any children?"

"Yes, three," the old lady said rather grimly and snapped her mouth shut like a purse.

"Don't you like them?"

"Don't see much of them. Two boys and a girl. All married now."

Lizzie took a deep breath and held it. This was the important bit.

"And have they got any children?"

"Yes, seven between them," Mrs Peabody said shortly.

Lizzie could have cried. She wouldn't want any more grandchildren with seven already!

"What's the matter, child, aren't you feeling well?"

"Not very," admitted Lizzie, "now that I know you're a grandmother."

"Good gracious, what difference does that make? Don't you like grandmothers?"

"I don't know, I haven't got any. My friend Lucy goes to stay with hers."

"Does she get 'spoiled rotten'? Such an ugly phrase, but it's very expressive."

"I don't know about the rotten bit, but I think so. It sounds great the way she tells it."

"Ah well, perhaps hers is good at being a grandmother."

"Aren't you?" Lizzie asked, with some surprise.

"I've absolutely no idea. I've never seen any of my grandchildren. Two are in New Zealand, another pair are in Hong Kong and three are in Canada. And I can't afford to go traipsing round the world to see them, much as I'd like to. I remember all their birthdays, of course, and send them little things for Christmas, but I have to post them in October so it doesn't feel the same."

Lizzie's spirits lifted. "Mrs Peabody, would you be my granny? By adoption?"

"Me? I'd be no good as a granny. And I'm too old to learn…"

"No you're not. You could practise on me, so you'd be an expert when you see your real grandchildren."

Mrs Peabody swivelled round on the bench and stared at Lizzie. "What an extraordinary suggestion. Do you really think I'd do?"

Lizzie considered carefully. "Yes," she said slowly, "I really think you'd do."

"Help, Phone the Police"

"I really ought to meet your mother first, Lizzie," Mrs Peabody said. "She might not like the idea of you coming home with a new granny. Incidentally, have you told her anything about this?"

"Not exactly," admitted Lizzie. "I'm not really allowed to talk to strangers, but you looked different. I wanted to get it right first, before I mentioned it to Mum."

Mrs Peabody laughed. "Your mother must have a strong constitution. The introduction of a new member into a family surely deserves more than a 'mention', Lizzie. It might even come as a bit of a shock! Now, when would be a good time to visit your mother?"

"Sunday evening. Mum's at work during the week. She drives a minibus all round this part of the city, up as far as the hospital, and back past my school. She's very good at it, but she gets awfully tired. Come tomorrow evening and I'll tell her."

"*Ask* her, don't *tell* her," Mildred Peabody said firmly. Must have been a teacher, Lizzie thought regretfully, and she wondered what Lucy's granny had been.

Lizzie didn't tell her mother what the visit was all about, she just asked if a friend could come over on Sunday evening.

"Not if you're going to raise the roof together, Lizzie. I'll have just got the place straight by then, and I'd like it to last."

"Oh no, Mum, she's not that sort. She's a little bit older than most of my friends, and *very* sensible."

So Lizzie's mum was expecting somebody

of about twelve or thirteen when she opened the door to Mrs Peabody. And as the real reason for the visit emerged, Lizzie's mum went very still. Then her face began to go dull red. Even her ears and the back of her neck turned red, and her eyes were stonier than Lizzie had ever seen them.

"If you'll excuse us for a moment, I'd like a word with my daughter," she said stiffly. "In the kitchen, Lizzie, and then…"

Mrs Peabody realized instantly that Lizzie had not discussed the plan with her mother and that she herself was now in the middle of a decidedly sticky situation. With a brief reproachful glance at Lizzie who was backing away towards the kitchen, she said, "Mrs Giles, I'm so sorry. This is obviously rather a shock. Why don't I take myself off for a little walk and let you discuss it, and then perhaps I could pop back later and see how things are … I mean, er, well, Lizzie may have changed her mind, or … or something," she ended lamely.

"Why don't you do just that?" Mrs Giles snapped nastily, opening the front door, and almost pushing Mrs Peabody out. Mrs Peabody backed out fast, and the door banged shut in her face.

Mrs Giles stormed into the kitchen and rounded on Lizzie. "How many times have I told you never, *ever* to talk to strangers when you're by yourself? And then giving someone your address and inviting them back here! Have you gone mad? Don't you ever listen to the news, Lizzie, and hear the dreadful things that some people do to children when they get them on their own? I must have told you a hundred times already and they tell you exactly the same at school. What about that policeman who came to your class and showed you those films? He wasn't doing it for fun, if that's what you all thought."

"Mum," wailed Lizzie, "it wasn't like that at all! She didn't talk to me first, *I* spoke to her..." Her voice trailed away as she realized her mistake.

"You went up to a perfect stranger?" Mrs Giles asked in a strangled voice. "Lizzie, do you think people wear badges on their coats telling you whether they are going to be nasty or not? You can't tell – that's the whole point. You can't tell just by looking."

She scooped some crumbs off the table automatically and threw them into the sink, banging her hands down on to the draining board. She stood with her back to Lizzie, shoulders hunched up to her ears. Then she said softly, almost to herself, "If anything happened to you, I'd never forgive myself. But I can't be there all the time. Children have to learn to go out alone and take care of themselves. All I can do is warn you. Over and over again, until you can warn yourself. Awful things do happen sometimes and often it's just forgetfulness – one mistake – that's all it takes."

Her voice faded away but she still stood there gripping the edge of the sink as if it might fall off, her head bent right down.

By this time Lizzie was crying too.

"Mum, I know what you've always told me, but it really wasn't like that."

Mrs Giles suddenly wheeled round, and grabbed a wooden chair.

"Right. You sit down there and tell me exactly what *did* happen. Then I'm phoning the police, and they can come and pick up that woman when she comes back. *If* she comes back, which is highly unlikely. She'll be miles away by now, in a car with her accomplices, planning the next kidnapping or burglary!"

"Mum, Mum, please stop," Lizzie pleaded

despairingly, crumpling into a chair opposite her mother, who watched her coldly.

She did her best to explain it all clearly and her mum did her best to listen very carefully, but it was difficult for both of them.

"There were lots of other people around," Lizzie ended defensively. "Anyway, I'd already worked out I could run faster than her and we weren't even sitting close together. There was miles of space between us. She couldn't even have reached me."

Mum leaned forward on her elbows and grabbed Lizzie's wrists. "All right, it wasn't quite as bad as it sounded at first. But it was a terrible risk, and I'm still shocked. It's quite hard taking care of you all by myself, and when I'm at work I just have to trust you to be sensible. We're new here, and until we make friends there's nobody else to help."

Lizzie almost said, "Well, we're not going to make many friends if we're not allowed to talk to anyone, are we?" but she swallowed the thought before it leaked out of her mouth.

"I didn't realize you wanted a granny so badly. It's that wretched Lucy's fault, with all her gloating. But there must be another way of doing it. We'll think of a better way together, Lizzie, because that Mrs Pea ... Peaperson won't be back. You can be sure of that!"

"She was really nice," muttered Lizzie, realizing just how much she had liked Mrs Peabody now she had gone.

Mrs Giles shoved a box of paper tissues towards Lizzie, and took a handful herself. Still sniffling, she filled the kettle, plugged it in and dropped teabags into two mugs. The doorbell rang. Lizzie stared at her mother.

"It's her. She's back!" she whispered.

"Heaven help us, what do we do now?" breathed Mum nervously.

Lizzie went to open the door.

Mrs Peabody smiled at her, but made no attempt to come in. She held out a postcard towards Mrs Giles, who was hovering just behind Lizzie.

"You probably want to forget the whole idea, Mrs Giles, but I've written my name, address and phone number here. I've lived in Barrow Lane for almost thirty years now and before I retired I was Deputy Head at the Girls' High School. Of course it's the Comprehensive now. But a lot of people know me round here, so I've put some names and phone numbers on the card in case you'd like to contact them. Please do – I'm sure they wouldn't mind. And possibly we might meet again, eh, Lizzie?" She smiled warmly and turned to go.

"I'm s-sorry," Mrs Giles and Lizzie stammered in unison.

"No damage done. And you can't be too careful." Mrs Peabody waved a knobbly hand, as she walked towards the stairwell.

Mrs Giles shook her head violently, as if trying to rearrange her thoughts, and then called along the corridor, in a twisted-up voice, "Erm … won't you come in and have a cup of tea before you go? I was jumping to conclusions a bit."

So Mrs Peabody came back to the flat. It felt very uncomfortable at first, but over tea and garibaldi biscuits she told them about herself, her family and her little house on the canal. Mrs Giles hoped her face didn't look as blotchy as Lizzie's. Lizzie was watching her mother and thought that laughing helped.

And Mrs Peabody was certainly making them laugh about the things her friends might say about her, when Mrs Giles "checked her references".

The atmosphere improved minute by minute and Lizzie couldn't believe that only half an hour ago her mum had been raging and shouting at her. Already they had accepted an invitation to tea at Barrow Lane next week, and now Mrs Peabody was saying, "I believe that in real adoptions there is a probationary period. Would it be a good idea for us to have one too? After all, I may not come up to scratch. Lucy's granny sounds fierce competition and Lizzie might well change her mind. I am totally inexperienced after all."

"So is Lizzie," Mrs Giles laughed. "She may turn out to be the sort of grandchild you would be happy to lose in the nearest fog. Have you thought of that, Liz?"

As Mrs Peabody was getting ready to go and Mrs Giles was helping her on with her coat, she said, "Do phone those numbers, Mrs Giles, and don't be too hard on Lizzie. I know how worried you must have been, but I do like her enterprise. Loads of initiative."

At school the next day Lizzie said to Lucy, "Going to tea at my gran's on Thursday."

"Thought you didn't have one. You said you didn't."

"Well I have. She lives in Barrow Lane."

"Oh, one of my grans lives in a cottage in the middle of orchards in the country and the other one lives in a big house near the sea."

"I know all that. It's nice to have one just around the corner though. Handy for visiting."

"But I thought you said… Oh, there's Becky – I hope she's brought my tracksuit back," and Lucy ran off to catch Becky.

Gran Gets
It Wrong

Mrs Giles *did* contact the people Mrs Peabody had suggested, just to be on the safe side.

"I spent the whole of my lunch hour on the phone, Lizzie. That doctor I thought would be at his surgery turned out to be a doctor of Molecular Biology at the University. And *he* turned out to be a 'she'!"

Mrs Giles was stirring eggs in a pan while Lizzie was making some toast.

"And then I tried that vicar. And he turned out to be the Dean of the Cathedral! I almost dropped the phone. Didn't know whether to call him 'Sir' or 'Your Worship' or what. It was all like that. Your Mrs Peabody certainly has friends in high places. This is just about scrambled, have you finished the buttering?"

"Yes, it's ready. But what did they *say* about her?" Lizzie asked anxiously.

"Well, it was all a bit embarrassing. By the time I'd explained what it was about, they started laughing. And the vicar couldn't stop. It was like a disease." She sat down, cut a square of toast, and arranged a precise square of egg on top of it. "They all seem to think she's batty but harmless. Hoped you'd both enjoy yourselves, and that you like surprises, Lizzie. Why would they say a thing like that?"

"No idea. But does that mean we can have this trial – to see if it works?"

"Well, I suppose so. Can't see anything wrong with an invitation to tea."

But then Mrs Giles's shift work was unexpectedly changed, so she had to ring Mrs Peabody to tell her that only Lizzie would be coming. Mrs Peabody admitted she was relieved.

"I'm in a flat spin about it already, Mrs Giles. I don't know what the child expects, but I'll never be able to live up to it. And there aren't any evening classes to learn how to be a proper granny! So if I have to improvise suddenly, I'd rather do it without an audience."

Mrs Giles sympathized. "I don't really know what she expects, either. In the books she reads, grannies tend to be little old ladies who live in little old cottages and grow all their own vegetables. Oh, and they always have white hair done up in a bun and wear old-fashioned clothes and a shawl and walk with a stick. Useful for poking parsnips with, I suppose. And I think they make gingerbread and parkin, or is that the same thing? Yes, and get their water from a pump in the garden."

"This is going to be ghastly! I suppose I could throw a bucket into the canal and pretend it was a well. But nobody in their right mind would drink it!"

"Good luck," laughed Mrs Giles, and went back to work.

When Lizzie arrived at Barrow Lane, number twenty-seven looked very small. The whole terrace was built of dingy red bricks with purple slate roofs. Each house had frilly ridge-tiles, one chimney and a bay window. Each house had a tiny patch of garden in front, with a path of patterned tiles leading from a curly iron gate to the front door. Every front door had a stained glass window set

into the upper half. It reminded Lizzie of one of those puzzles where you have to spot the differences between almost identical pictures.

Mrs Peabody answered the doorbell and invited her in. She looked older today than Lizzie remembered and she walked with a stick. A crocheted shawl hung unevenly from her bony shoulders and she wore a rather long skirt. Lizzie followed her through a little hallway splattered with blobs of coloured light from the stained glass, and into the kitchen at the back of the house.

"Oh," Lizzie said with pleasure when she saw the table, "it looks like a party. We only ever have tablecloths for parties, and that's the only time we ever make three-cornered sandwiches."

A rocking-chair filled up most of the space in the little kitchen, and Mrs Peabody lowered herself awkwardly into it. At the same moment a ginger cat leaped across the floor with a squawk and lurked under the table, watching Lizzie warily.

"You'll have to learn to keep your tail out of the way of those rockers, Pusskin. Now, where's my knitting and my specs? My legs are playing up a bit today, Lizzie dear, so I didn't do any baking, I'm afraid. I had to buy a loaf instead."

"We always have thick-sliced at home, and then it's best for toast. Gran." She added as an afterthought. The word felt strange in her mouth.

"Come and sit here, child." Mrs Peabody patted a small stool near her chair. Lizzie obediently sat down and for once couldn't think of anything to say. Mrs Peabody's glasses were the half-moon sort with thin gold frames, making her look more like an ancient headmistress than ever. Lizzie couldn't remember her wearing them before. Perhaps she only used them for knitting but they didn't seem to help much, for Lizzie noticed that Mrs Peabody had dropped several stitches.

The cat returned and sat near Lizzie's feet, allowing itself to be stroked. Then it wandered away, jumped up on to the draining board and began to lap from a small porcelain jug.

At this, Mrs Peabody gave an undignified shriek, and managed an awkward, almost vertical take-off from the depths of the rocking-chair. The chair pivoted sideways, knocking Lizzie off the stool. Mrs Peabody grabbed the table to stop herself falling over Lizzie, but did so nevertheless, and an absolute avalanche of crockery slid down the tablecloth clutched in Mrs Peabody's fingers. The noise was stupendous as plates shattered and cups exploded on the tiles. Both of them sprawled on the floor, covered with cloth, crocheted shawl, bits of broken china, puddles of blackberry jam and milk, and bent and battered sandwiches.

Lizzie felt like crying. Everything was ruined. When she lifted a corner of the tablecloth she thought Mrs Peabody really *was* crying. Tears dripped down her nose, her face was all red and screwed up and the most extraordinary noise was coming from her wide open mouth.

Then she realized that Mrs Peabody was positively cackling with laughter! A jam and crumb-covered hand patted Lizzie's knee.

"Oh, that's taught me a lesson, Lizzie. I'll never do all that again, not even for you."

The cackles continued with gasps and snorts in between, as Mrs Peabody sat up with half a cress sandwich sticking to one of her shoulders and her heel in a puddle of dark lumpy jam.

"Help me up, there's a dear, and don't look so distraught. Or are you hurt? At your age you're supposed to bounce." They both stood up and checked each other.

"No bones broken and not much blood. Apart from those blackberry pools on the

floor, of course. What a wreck of a tea-party
– there's hardly a thing left whole. Rescue
those buns, Lizzie, before you tread on them.
It's only the icing that's a bit squashed –
they're probably still edible. Now, let's find
the four corners of the tablecloth, pick up as
many bits as we can and throw them into the
middle of the cloth. I must say, whenever I do
something, I certainly do it thoroughly!"

She began laughing again as they dropped
bits of broken saucers, a teapot spout and the
handles of the sugar bowl on to the cloth. In
the end Lizzie couldn't help laughing too.

Then they carried the bulging, dripping, clanking bundle straight into the garden and dropped it into a king-size dustbin. Mrs Peabody slammed the rubber lid down hard.

It took them about twenty minutes to clear up the kitchen and another five to carry the dreadful rocking-chair back to a neighbour's where it belonged. Then Mrs Peabody made some tea and they had toast and marmalade and the remains of the iced buns.

"I *am* sorry, Lizzie, but I was trying so hard to be the kind of granny you'd read about in books. Didn't work though, did it? That wretched rocking-chair made me feel seasick, and I've hated that tea service for years, all those awful pink dandelions crawling round the plates. I got the shawl and the long skirt from Oxfam and I only ever use that stick for blackberrying. Oh Lizzie, do you realize it's going to be very hard work for you?"

"Why, Gran? I mean, what is?"

"You are going to have to teach me how to be a *real* granny!"

Manhunt

Lizzie had hidden her list inside her social studies notebook. She ticked the first entry – "1 Granny" – with great satisfaction, then decorated all round the edge of the paper with a neat design of three-cornered sandwiches and iced cupcakes with cherries on the top. It should really have been iced buns, but the cupcakes were a better shape to fit the pattern. And her new red felt-tip was just right for the cherries.

Mrs Peabody began visiting the flat quite regularly. "Could Lizzie come round after school to help me with a bit of … er … cooking?" That turned out to be brewing elderflower wine – bottles and bottles of it. Or, "If Lizzie isn't busy, would she like a game of cards?"

"I'm sure she'd love one." Mrs Giles was really pleased that Lizzie and her new granny were getting on so well. "She's got Snap and Happy Families, she can bring them with her." But Mrs Peabody had other ideas back at Barrow Lane.

"Let's have a game of poker. Sharpens your wits. If I teach you, you'll never be caught out in a poker game, Lizzie. Might save you a lot of trouble if you ever meet a cardsharp on a river-steamer!"

It was after the poker and just before a game of gin rummy that Lizzie said, absentmindedly, "Gran, next on my list is a grandpa. I must start looking."

Mrs Peabody's hands stopped in mid-shuffle. "A grandpa? Of course, everybody needs a grandpa! I wish my Sam were still alive, he'd have adopted you on the spot. Pneumonia got him in the end, before he'd seen any of his grandchildren. I still miss him a lot. But now Lizzie, where will you start searching?"

"Oh, I haven't really thought yet. I wondered if you could help. If you're not too busy of course. It shouldn't be difficult. There are always lots of men outside the Crown and Anchor and the betting shop and off-licence and there's always…" Her voice faded as she saw Mrs Peabody's scandalized expression. The cold disapproving voice reminded her of her mum's that evening when Lizzie had explained how she first met Mrs Peabody.

"Lizzie, stop it! And start using your brains.

Let's hear a few intelligent, *safe* suggestions!"

Lizzie gulped. Gran sounded really fierce. She thought hard. Then suggested hesitantly, "Well, what about the bowling green? All the men look just like grandfathers there, with white moustaches and Panama hats to match. Only they're always concentrating so hard you can never talk to them. Or what about the Co-op café? Mum and I go in there sometimes, and there are always lots of old men having tea and buns. It looks like a Senior Citizens' club sometimes."

Mrs Peabody put the cards away. "Both of those sound promising. If it's the Bowling Club, I'm sure I could get us in somehow. I have lots of contacts. Might even know one of the members... The Co-op idea might be quicker, though." They agreed to start there.

Lizzie and her gran went to the Co-op café for the next three Saturday mornings, making one cup of tea and one Pepsi last as long as possible. They always arrived early enough to choose an empty four-seater table near the window. Then Mrs Peabody used what she called "tactics". They piled coats and empty carrier bags on to the empty chairs and if a woman came towards their table looking for a seat, Gran would wave like a maniac to an imaginary friend in the queue. The women always walked past them then and found a place somewhere else. If, however, an elderly man came near, Gran would immediately whisk the bags and coats from one of the chairs and say invitingly, "There's a spare seat here. Can I hold your tray for you while you sit down?"

It always worked. Some of the men who joined them talked too much and some were almost silent. The ones Lizzie disliked most were the ones who brought out photographs of their grandchildren and expected her to admire them.

She soon discovered you couldn't always judge by appearances. One elderly man looked perfect – just like a film star grandfather – with silvery white hair and a nice tweedy suit. He pinched Lizzie's cheek playfully. It was a hard pinch and it hurt.

"I get on well with kiddies," he boasted to Mrs Peabody, puffing pipe smoke in her face. "I'm the Father Christmas in the grotto at Selfridges. Ho-ho-ho!" he boomed suddenly, as a demonstration. Everybody in the café went quiet and looked at their table. He also talked with his mouth full and soon everything was spattered with bits of sugary Eccles cake. Lizzie hated him and decided that if he tried to pinch her cheek again, she'd bite his fingers.

Another man joined them without asking.
He nibbled a chocolate biscuit inside his coat
collar and didn't drop any crumbs. He talked
softly and furtively; Lizzie thought he looked
as if he'd escaped from prison. He asked
Gran too many questions about her house,
then said urgently, "I'm looking for a room.
Clean and quiet. A kindly woman like you

would enjoy looking after a lodger. Company – and a bit of money, no questions asked."

Lizzie felt scared, but Mrs Peabody smiled warmly and said very sweetly, "Actually my granddaughter here spends a lot of time with me. She looks angelic now, but she's a terror in my house. A whole tea-service on the floor once and the noise...! And there *are* my seven other grandchildren..."

She winked wickedly, secretly, at Lizzie who leaned across the table and whispered loudly, "My granny drinks. Her spare room is full of bottles!"

Both the Father Christmas man and the escaped prisoner looked shocked, and left in a hurry. Gran and Lizzie watched them almost racing each other to the escalator. It was while they were still choking with giggles that quite the wrong sort of man joined them. He was big and his huge Icelandic sweater made him look even bigger. His hair was thick and only just beginning to go grey at the sides. The rest of it was curly and the colour of

conkers. Lizzie watched him take off a
camera and a pair of binoculars before he
could drink his coffee. Gran gave her the
money to get another Pepsi, a tea and two
Chelsea buns. Lizzie stood in the queue
thoughtfully. She hadn't decided exactly what
sort of grandpa she wanted, but she was
beginning to know the kind she didn't want.

Gran Gets
It Right

When she came back with the tray, Gran said,
"Lizzie, this is Ben Bailey. He lives in one of
those big old houses near the ring road with
his daughter and her family. And Lizzie, he's a
bird watcher too!"

Lizzie smiled politely, and began to nibble
her bun in rings from the outside. In that way
it stayed a Chelsea bun, just getting smaller
and smaller until it was doll-size. Gran and
Mr Bailey were chatting away like old
friends. He had glowing brown eyes and a
catching, kindly smile, Lizzie noticed, but
with five grandchildren already, living in part
of his house, he wouldn't be interested in

adopting another one. Why didn't Gran realize? From his outdoors look and smell, Lizzie guessed he'd be the sort of person who would spend hours happily lying in a ditch watching a lesser spotted wobble-throated warbler. She wished he would go, so that they could concentrate on the job in hand. But he and Gran seemed to be getting on well, and he didn't go. In fact Gran invited him back to Barrow Lane to explore the fishing in her bit of the canal. And he invited her back to his house to meet his family. Several times.

Mr Bailey now became a regular visitor at Gran's and Lizzie gradually stopped resenting him. But he was noisy! His explosive laugh made both Gran and Lizzie jump, before they joined in as well, and when it was too cold or wet to fish, he and Lizzie would mend things for Gran. When Lizzie's mum saw how well he fixed things, she brought her iron round and he soon stopped it squirting scalding water over everything. Then they had a supper party to celebrate and sang silly songs until midnight.

But every time Lizzie tried to remind Gran about the Bowling Club, she just said "Soon, soon", and promptly forgot. It was a most irritating habit. And Lizzie's list was not getting any shorter.

Then one Sunday afternoon, when Mr Bailey and Lizzie were trying to unblock a hoover hose and Gran was upstairs labelling her latest brew of tea-wine, Mr Bailey said, "Didn't know you weren't Mildred's real grandchild. Thought I'd spotted a likeness until she told me about you two adopting each other."

Lizzie stiffened, waiting for the explosive laugh. But it didn't come. Mr Bailey extricated a wodge of paper tissue that had been blocking the hose and held it out

triumphantly for inspection. Then he said
gently, "She also told me about you wanting
a grandfather. If you haven't anyone else in
mind, could I ... offer my services? I know it's
being a bit greedy but you don't often get the
chance to choose a new granddaughter."

"Would you, would you really?" Lizzie
asked excitedly. She could hardly
believe her luck.

"Why don't we try it for a bit? Like you and your gran? The only thing is Lizzie, I'd be bringing a bit of luggage with me. If you take me on, you'd have to take on my family too. That would mean a new auntie and uncle (that's my daughter Sue and her husband) and I suppose their five children would have to be, well – cousins. There are two girls older than you, a pair of twin boys about your age and a little girl of four. You'd better think it over, Lizzie – it's quite a lot to handle."

Lizzie's eyes shone but she managed to say very politely, "Oh, I think I could manage it, thank you, if *they* don't mind."

Then she raced into the hallway and yelled up the stairs, "Gran, Gran, you don't have to worry about the Bowling Club after all. I've got a new grandpa and he's just unblocked your hoover!"

*   *   *

At school the next day, Lizzie and Lucy were making a Viking long boat in papier mâché.

"We had supper at my gran's last night and Grandpa was there."

"But you said you didn't have a grandpa," objected Lucy, cutting out a cardboard shield.

"Well I do. He lives with my Auntie Sue and Uncle Brian. And there are five cousins. Hannah and Julia are older than us and Jamie and Davy are identical twins as long as they keep their mouths shut, because you can only tell them apart by their teeth, and Tabitha's the youngest."

"Wish I had cousins," Lucy said enviously, "for spending holidays with. Having a load of brothers and sisters isn't half as good, because they're always around, nicking things, and you can't ever get away from them."

"That's what I think," Lizzie said happily, though she hadn't thought of it before.

"Lizzie, I don't believe you. I think you're the biggest liar I know!"

*   *   *

While Mum was watching the news, Lizzie borrowed her bottle of Tippex, took her felt-tips and schoolbag into her room and closed the door firmly. Painting out the entries on her list for "1 brother" and "1 sister", Lizzie then blew it dry and carefully wrote "1 aunt and uncle" and underneath, "several cousins". Then she ticked both entries very proudly, even though she knew that Gran had actually engineered most of her new family.

She drew another border pattern just inside the line of cakes and sandwiches, a dancing pattern of boots, from Grandpa's fishing wellies to the little red wellies of a four year old. With ordinary ones and trendy ones and football boots (for the twins) in between. Lizzie admired the finished pattern and wondered whether she would be a professional border decorator when she grew up. Then she heard her mother switch off the TV, so she popped her notebook into its hiding place, and went to bed.

But her list was still not quite complete. There was still "a baby". And this time she was going to do it by herself.

The Mistake

Lizzie started looking for a baby in the pram park outside Kindercare. The shop had a small chained off pavement space just outside the big window and it was always full of buggies and prams on Saturdays. The smallest babies looked sweet, the bits you could see, but they didn't do enough to be very interesting, so Lizzie decided the bigger, sitting-up sort might be better value. She smiled at one or two but they just looked at her, like little puddings. So she tried pulling faces at them to make them laugh. They certainly stopped being puddings then. One started howling and set the others off, revving up like motorbikes. Lizzie stared at

them in horror and tried to tickle the nearest
one's tummy to show she was only playing.

"Get your hands off of him!"

"You leave her alone!"

"What do you think you're up to?"

Lizzie looked up to find a mob of angry
mothers all shouting at her.

"I was only *looking* at them … well, only
playing with them…" But nobody listened to
her. Hands were unbuckling safety harnesses
and grabbing babies, plucking children out of
their nests and clutching them tightly. All she
could see were wide open mouths, gobbling
at her. "I wasn't trying to steal them, if that's

what you're thinking. And I haven't got
measles or anything..." Lizzie hurriedly
backed away, and fell over the little white
chains. Scrambling up, she ran. Away from
the shouting mothers, away from the howling
babies, into Littlewoods and out on to the
other side of the precinct.

She sat by the fountain to cool her face.
Stupid women, she thought crossly. She had
gone right off babies. Obviously it was going
to be harder to find a baby than it had been
finding a granny or grandpa, because you had
to get the mother's permission first. And even
the most gorgeous baby might have an
appalling mum. Perhaps the pram park was
the wrong place to start with. Perhaps a baby
clinic would have been better...

Lizzie felt a faint pull on her anorak, looked round and saw a small boy wiping his face on her coat.

"Hey you, I'm not a Kleenex!" she began angrily. Then she remembered what it felt like to be shouted at and asked more gently, "Haven't you got a hankie?"

The little boy just stared at her with his mouth open and his nose running. "Use this then," she said, fishing a clean tissue out of her pocket. He made no attempt to take it and she guessed he probably didn't know how to use it. Lizzie wiped his nose for him, not very well, as she had never wiped anyone

else's nose before. His face was so grubby that tide marks showed where she had mopped up. His jumper was three sizes too big for him; the sleeves were rolled up firmly, round and round like doughnuts and his little arms stuck through the holes.

"You are pretty disgusting," Lizzie said in a friendly voice.

The little boy looked at her, smiled, and offered her a sweet. It was a fruit gum, stuck to his palm and furred with fluff.

"You keep it," she said kindly. To her horror he slapped his hand over his mouth and hoovered it up. Lizzie blinked as she thought of all the germs.

"Haven't I seen you before in the playground near the flats? With some big kids? Ginger hair like yours, only darker? D'you live near here?"

The small boy began nodding his head like one of those toy dogs in the rear window of cars. He only stopped when a strident voice sliced through the precinct, "Mac, where are you? Didn't I tell you not to wander off?"

Lizzie groaned inside. Was the whole precinct full of angry mums? A large woman hurried towards them, frowning fiercely and carrying a spiteful-looking gardening fork.

She looked as if she had been made out of grey plasticine and dressed in jumble sale clothes. Thick veins bubbled purple up her pallid bare legs.

"I been looking for you everywhere, you little stinker!"

Lizzie stood up nervously, prepared to defend the small boy. He was sweet-sucking noisily and didn't seem at all scared by the menacing figure.

"We were only having a little chat together," Lizzie explained nervously.

"That's lies for starters, 'cause he don't talk," the grey face said loudly. "Can't get a word out of him, *unlike* the others who never stop. It's all or nothing with my lot." She looked Lizzie up and down, but Lizzie couldn't decide what she was thinking.

"He shouldn't've gone off like that. He'll get himself lost one day."

"Nice little boy, isn't he?" Lizzie heard herself saying nervously, "Is his name Mike?"

"No, Mac. When he come along we'd run

short of names, after all the others. *He* was a Mistake! So I asked the kids what their best name was and they said McDonald's. He gets called Mac for short but it's really McDonald."

Lizzie looked at Mac with renewed sympathy. His nose was running again, but she didn't dare offer him the tissue. She was a bit afraid of his mum.

"I'd better be going. Bye, Mac. See you in the playground sometime."

"Thanks for minding him, then," Mac's mother said surprisingly.

Lizzie ran all the way home.

Her mother was putting some shopping away.

"Mum, I found this little lost boy in the precinct. Actually, he found me and he's called Mac. But his mother was *awful!*"

"Mac short for McDonald? I know that family. Or some of them anyway. They're the Ryans, live in one of the other blocks – Arundel, I think. Mrs Ryan comes on my bus

Thursday afternoons and goes to their allotment on the other side of the canal. She's always got some kids with her, all redheads, and I've heard her calling the little one 'Mac'."

"Ryans?" Lizzie remembered hearing warnings about a Ryan family at school. But nobody could be frightened of such a little boy. Perhaps it was a different family, or she'd got the wrong name. Anyway, it was Mac she was concerned about. Mac and his alarming mother.

"She also called him a *Mistake*! I think that's awful, right in front of him. And the poor little thing was filthy, and can't talk. He ought to be talking by now … and…"

Mrs Giles suddenly looked alarmed.

"Lizzie, if you're thinking of adopting Mac, then you can forget it. Fast. The Ryans would resent it like anything. She does her best poor woman, looking after eight of them, and none of them seem to go hungry. Can you imagine what it must be like, to have ten people living in a flat like this? I don't know how she manages at all. So you just steer clear, Lizzie, I mean it."

So Lizzie went to her bedroom, closed the door and found her social studies notebook. She took out her list and an indelible pen and drew a thick black line through "and a baby". She sat back on her heels and tried to work out whether she was a failure, or just showing common sense. Either way she still felt sad about abandoning Mac.

When she went to bed her mum came in, and sat on the end.

"Lizzie, there are alternatives to adoption. Other options, I mean, like fostering and befriending. Fostering is when you look after a child for a short time, because everyone knows the child will be going back to the real parents as soon as possible. Befriending is where you take care of somebody but they don't necessarily come to live with you. You make a special friend of them and … well … look after that person in particular.

"Why don't you become a Befriender to Mac, Lizzie? You sounded as if you liked him, in spite of his grubbiness. So why not just talk to him when you see him in the playground, or give him a push on the swings? Or just listen if he tries to talk. Tell you what, why not give him one of your old picture books – a new-looking one and write in the front, 'To Mac from Lizzie'? And put your address in it as well. Then he will know it's a present specially for him and his mum will know where it's come from and with luck no one will be upset."

Lizzie smiled to herself in the dark. She had often thought of her mum as being a bit like a beige cushion – comfortable but unexciting. Lucy's mum, who was more red-satin-with-tassels, would never have let her Lucy go near a child like Mac, in case she caught nits. Now here was her mum actually suggesting a marvellous way round the problem.

"Thanks, Mum, it's a great idea. D'you know, I bet I'm the youngest Befriender in the world? *Guinness Book of Records*, here I come!"

"Don't let it go to your head, Lizzie. And watch out, that's all."

A Spot of Bother

Lizzie chose her favourite Wombles book for Mac, wrote inside it carefully and wrapped it in shiny green paper. She kept watch from her balcony high above the playground and the next time she spotted the small figure ambling past the swings she ran down to find him. He was playing behind the benches, digging holes in the ground with a wooden lolly-stick. A crowd of red-headed children were tormenting some boys on the swings a long way away off. Those must be his brothers and sisters, Lizzie thought briefly.

"Hello, Mac. This is for you to take home and show your mum."

He looked up at her and smiled, then took the parcel and began tearing off the green paper excitedly.

"D'you like the Wombles?"

Mac nodded eagerly and began to sing the Wombles song, with "Ner, ner, ner" instead of the proper words. But he sang the tune perfectly. Then he stopped suddenly in mid "ner" and began stuffing the half-unwrapped parcel inside his anorak.

"Oh, can't I read you a bit now?" Lizzie asked disappointedly as the little boy struggled to pull up his zip. Then she heard it, the piercing, demon shrieks and pounding feet of his brothers and sisters.

"See you, Mac. Enjoy the book," Lizzie whispered hurriedly, edging behind the nearest bushes. She wanted to avoid any meeting with the other Ryan children as such meetings, she had noticed, generally ended in a fight. It was the thing they seemed to be best at and because all seven of them always stuck together, they always won. She made a

point of disappearing whenever they came near. It just seemed sensible.

The next time Lizzie saw Mac he was making a road out of matchsticks and pebbles, grubbing out any bits of grass that got in the way. The rest of the Ryans were testing the roundabout to destruction, pushing the circular metal plate round so fast it was screaming in its cast-iron sleeve. She squatted down beside him.

"Like the book, Mac? Look what I found in a car boot sale. Didn't cost much because it's a bit scratched, but it's all there and everything works." She brought a little toy ambulance out of her pocket, and put it on Mac's road.

Mac smiled happily, his eyes shining, and

began making loud siren noises, "Der-der. Der-der". Lizzie showed him how to open the back doors and pull out a tiny stretcher; and she talked to him about hospitals and accidents, and dialling 999. Mac listened intently, then looked up at her and said very slowly and carefully, "Am-lance".

Lizzie hugged him with delight, and Mac laughed proudly.

"You can stop that for starters. Let him go. Now!" a cold, grating voice commanded, above Lizzie's head. Startled, she overbalanced backwards and sprawled on the grass. Red-haired Ryans surrounded her. Mac had vanished.

"He's not allowed to talk to strangers," the oldest girl said nastily. "Specially when they try giving him things." She tossed the little ambulance to one of her brothers.

Lizzie stood up awkwardly, and tried to explain. "Mac'll tell you..." she began stupidly, before realizing of course that Mac could tell them nothing.

"We take care of him see, and no one else lays a finger on him," the oldest girl said threateningly. Lizzie took a step backwards and opened her mouth to apologize. "Who are you shoving?" another voice said spitefully, too near the back of her neck.

Hands pushed her roughly from behind. The big girl flicked her fingers at Lizzie's face, as if flicking peas off a table. It stung, and Lizzie put up her hands to protect her face.

Then the others began flicking. She stumbled forwards, while fingers prodded, pinched and pulled her. Hard shoes kicked her legs and tripped her feet. She moved blindly, arms over her head to ward off the hobgoblin fingers, crouched down, hoping to push her way into a clear space. But the Ryans shoved her back, jostling her from one to the other, grabbing her shoulders and twisting her round, pulling her hair and flicking like wasp stings. She tried to shout, but each attempt was drowned by excited shrieks and screams of laughter. It was a nightmare. Lizzie realized that anybody looking would see only a mob of children laughing and dodging round. No one would guess there was a terrified victim in the middle of the swirling huddle.

They were moving across the grass quite fast now, like some demon's dance, when the oldest girl, clearly the leader, yelled out in her scratchy, gravelly voice, "And what do we do with rubbish?"

"We shove it in the bin!" the others

shrieked triumphantly, as if it was all part of a familiar game. Poor Lizzie, recoiling from the thumps and kicks and spiteful pinches, had no time or breath to do anything but try to keep her balance when suddenly they stopped her. She heard a heavy bolt being drawn back and the creak of a hinge. Then she was shoved violently from behind. She was in darkness. Doors clanged behind her, the bolt rattled.

As the shouts of laughter and clatter of footsteps faded into silence, Lizzie stood paralysed with shock. She knew where she was. In one of the dustbin dens. Each tower block had one – a concrete room about the size of a garage. Only many of the tenants didn't bother to use bins, but stuffed their rubbish into plastic carrier bags or cardboard boxes, which leaked and split, spilling the contents across the floor.

The stench was foul and when at last Lizzie dared to move, the floor was slimy and her feet crunched egg shells and squashed lumps of teabags. She sat down on the nearest rubber dustbin lid and pulled up her feet, trying to make herself as small as possible. Her eyes were getting used to the darkness now, and she could see pale pencil lines of light round the boarded up panes in the door. Vandals had broken the glass so often that the maintenance men stopped bothering to replace it and had just nailed heavy boards over them instead. Even as she watched, the lines grew darker, as outside dusk deepened.

The silence was terrifying. Everyone else had gone home for tea and would now be closing curtains and switching on lights and televisions. Even if Lizzie shouted, no one could hear – the ground floor of all the blocks was used only for the plumbing and heating systems. Besides, a Ryan might have been left on guard outside.

It was freezing and Lizzie pushed her hands inside her sleeves to warm them. Her mum wouldn't start worrying for ages, thinking she was probably with Lucy or Gran, and even then she'd wait too long before phoning, in case people thought she was fussing or over-anxious.

Lizzie strained her ears listening for rats. People had often seen rats in the dustbin dens and she could feel them waiting for her in the dark. She stiffened when she heard a soft noise, a shuffling, slithery sound. She held her breath, but her heart was thumping so loudly she couldn't hear properly. Then she realized the noise was *outside*. Shuffling footsteps outside. Lizzie opened her mouth to shout, but only an unrecognizable wobbly squeak came out, which somehow frightened her even more. Then she heard the bolt being drawn back and she toppled off the dustbin lid, stumbling towards the door.

Strong, onion-smelling fingers caught her just before she fell, and something warm and soft wrapped itself round her legs.

"Bunions and blisters," a voice said, making the words sound like swearing. "So he *was* right all along! Whatever are you doing in there? Some silly game, shouldn't wonder, but my lot is all inside with their dad, or I'd skin 'em alive. Mac kept pulling me and pulling me, even when I'd smacked him one, so I had to come and see what he was on about."

Lizzie discovered that it was Mac wrapped round her legs, and that it was his mother holding a feeble torch. She began to cry with relief.

"You the girl that gave him that book? The one I seen in the precinct weeks ago? Nice of

you. I've had
to read it over
and over to him.
You poor little thing,
you smell horrible. You
get off home and into a
bath, the germs in these dens
must be hopping. You could've
been in there all night if it hadn't been for
Mac. He's got brains all right even if he can't
talk."

"Thank you, *thank you*, Mac," cried Lizzie
and she hugged him tightly. Mrs Ryan saw
Lizzie to the lift and watched her press the
seventh button.

"You'll be all right now, won't you? See
you." Then she hoisted Mac on to her hip,
and waddled off into the darkness.

A Bit of Bravery

In the lift Lizzie looked forward to supper and sympathy. She hurt all over and in the dim light she could see bleeding scratches and bruises on her hands and legs. She wondered what on earth Mum would say. "Told you so" most likely, before putting her into an antiseptic bath that would make her smell just as awful, though in a different way. As she opened the front door she heard her mother's voice, higher than usual and tight with anxiety, talking on the phone.

"But we've settled down so well here, Alan. Lizzie likes her school and has made some real friends, and I've got a really good job at last. It wouldn't make sense to move away now. Why Arran anyway? What's so special about Arran?"

Lizzie felt as if her legs had turned to spaghetti and leaned against the wall for support. It was her dad. Wanting them to move again. Again! Just when she had found Lucy and Gran and Grandpa and all the cousins. She forgot the Ryan family in this new disaster.

"Running a bed and breakfast place in the summer is all very well, but what do we do all winter?" her mother was saying worriedly.

Hot tears of anger spilled down Lizzie's face. Why was her mum so *reasonable* all the time? Why didn't she just say "No" and put the phone down? That was the only way with Dad, when he got one of his famous ideas. Lizzie knew where Arran was. She had an old wooden jigsaw of the British Isles, and Arran was her favourite piece, a green island off the left hand of Scotland, only one piece away from Glasgow.

Lizzie couldn't face going into the kitchen to hear the news of yet another move and the thought of having to pack everything all over again. She thought Mum and Dad separating had stopped all that. Were they getting back together again? Stumbling out of the flat, she tumbled down the stairs down, down, down, trying to run away from this new nightmare. She ran all the way to Barrow Lane and pounded on the coloured glass of Gran's front door.

Mrs Peabody was marvellous. Recovering quickly from the shock of seeing Lizzie in such a state, she tucked her into a baggy, saggy old armchair in front of the fire, and made her a cup of hot chocolate. Then she listened to a most confusing story of dustbins and islands.

"Well," she said, when Lizzie had run out of breath, "first I'm going to phone your mother to let her know you're with me, before she goes frantic. I'll ask her if you can stay to supper, then that will give us time to get you clean and patched up before she sees you." Mrs Giles, struggling with the latest problem, sounded relieved to know where Lizzie was and gladly agreed to let her stay.

Then Gran collected an assortment of sticking plasters, cotton wool, antiseptic cream, towels and a bowl of warm water and began sponging Lizzie's cuts and bruises very gently. Questions about the injuries could wait for the moment, she decided, and thought it better to start with last things first this evening. "Wouldn't you like to go to Arran? An island might be rather fun after all, and you'd certainly get to know everybody quickly."

"No, I don't want to move ever again!" Lizzie wailed. "Me and Mum are all right here and I've got you and Grandpa and Lucy and everybody! I'd like to see Dad more often, but honestly Gran, he has got itchy feet. He wouldn't last six months on an island and as soon as he got bored, we'd have to be off again. He actually likes moving round all

the time, getting new jobs and looking for somewhere to live, not minding if it's horrible because then he can get busy with another move. It's exciting to begin with, but after a bit you hate it. Do you know Gran, this is my eleventh school? Mum and I have had enough!"

"I think he's going to be disappointed this time. I believe you have to sign a five-year lease on those flats and I know how much your mother likes her job. She was telling me all about her 'regulars' on the bus. Your mum will dig her heels in, if I know her. So I don't think there's any real danger of another move yet Lizzie, if neither of you wants to go. No, it's the other problem that's bothering me.

Those Ryan children are heading for real trouble. They're behaving like pack-animals – in the worst sense of course, not like a well-disciplined team working together sensibly – more like a mob. And mobs want excitement, but don't think of consequences. What are you going to do about Mac? Probably best to forget him, with that gang of mini-terrorists on your tail."

Mrs Peabody carefully inspected Lizzie to see if she had missed any injuries, then cleared away the towels, bowl and cotton wool. "You'll survive," she said kindly, patting her gently between two bruises, on her way to the kitchen.

Lizzie had been tempted to say bravely "I'm not afraid of *them*!" but she quickly realized that she was very much afraid, and being ambushed on the way home from school was a real possibility. Even with Lucy they would stand no chance against seven Ryans. She suddenly felt very angry at the injustice of it all.

Mrs Peabody brought in two mugs of hot tomato soup, and the toaster, which she plugged in near Lizzie's chair.

"Gran, it's not fair. Mac likes me and I was teaching him things. He was trying to talk to me. And his mum doesn't seem to mind. She looks funny and she shouts a lot, but I think she's friendly underneath."

Lizzie popped a slice of bread into the toaster and gazed down into it, thinking. The hot filaments looked like bright orange knitting, and the heat prickled her eyelashes. Then she faced Gran and said fiercely, "I'm going round to see his mum. When they're *all* there. And I'll ask her in front of them if I can take Mac out. For a walk or something. And if she says yes, they won't dare touch me again!"

"Sounds like stepping into a lion's den, Lizzie. Shall I come with you?"

"No thanks. They might think it was because I was too scared to go by myself."

Mrs Peabody took Lizzie home. When her

mum opened the door she looked shocked at
all the plasters and bruises, but before she
could ask what had happened, Gran said
lightly, "Had to do a bit of first-aid on Lizzie,
I'm afraid, Mrs Giles. Roller-skates are
downright dangerous, don't you think? I've
told Lizzie they ought to be banned." She
winked secretly at Lizzie, who was trying to
work out whether this was lying or not.
Anyway, Mrs Giles assumed Lizzie had been
roller-skating with Lucy, and then started
talking about Dad's phone call and Arran,
while Lizzie helped make coffee. Gran was

turning out to be a great partner, a real ally.

Lizzie found the Ryans' flat the very next Sunday. And what she had dreaded most happened. It was the stony-faced, gritty-voiced oldest girl who opened the door.

"Can I talk to your mum, please?" Lizzie asked in a clear, carrying voice. She hoped she didn't look as terrified as she felt, but she couldn't stop her heart from battering wildly. The big girl mumbled something, and was about to close the door, when Mac appeared, with a squeal of pleasure and wedged his solid little body against it.

"Get that door closed Arlene, letting all the heat out. Who is it anyway?"

Mrs Ryan appeared, with a half-eaten piccalilli sandwich in one hand. Seeing Lizzie, she flapped the sandwich at her, clearly inviting her in.

It was the untidiest kitchen Lizzie had ever seen. Full of people and full of things. All the people were eating. Bacon sandwiches mostly, but you could see why nobody sat round the table. The table was home for a hamster cage and a tank of goldfish, as well as being a dumping ground for mending, old batteries, crumpled comics and things growing in jars. Mr Ryan was shovelling a mountain of jeans into a washing machine, holding his sandwich between his teeth when he needed both hands. He smiled at her, over the heads of three of the smaller boys, who were pouring marbles down a home-made cardboard chute. It was so noisy it drowned the telly in the corner.

When Lizzie came in, all the children fell silent, watching her warily. They even stopped chewing, though their cheeks still bulged with the last mouthful. Lizzie was aware that plenty of bruises and sticking plaster still showed. Suddenly she knew that they were all afraid of *her*! Afraid that for the first time, one of their victims had come round to complain. She felt a brief flash of triumph, then remembered why she had come.

"Mr and Mrs Ryan, would you mind if … I mean … could I take Mac for a walk one day? Perhaps just along the towpath to see all the narrow boats, if he likes boats. One Saturday, I was thinking of … and we could take some bread for the swans. They're very greedy, but it's quite safe if you don't go too near the bank."

Mac stood beside her, patting her leg and smiling hopefully. Clearly he understood every word. Mrs Ryan looked at him proudly.

"That's an idea, Lizzie, and he loves boats, don't you, Mac? Tell you what, I'll find his old reins for you – it's safer near water and he does run off. Just till you're used to him."

Lizzie turned to Arlene, as she was the boss of the children, and said sweetly, "Are you sure you don't mind? After all, Mac is your brother. I haven't got any brothers or sisters, so it would be nice to borrow one occasionally, that is, if you really don't mind."

Arlene's pale face flushed deeply.

"Oh no, we don't mind, do we? Give us a rest for once."

Lizzie didn't even bother to try the lift. It was usually out of order anyway. She bounced like a ping-pong ball down all the stairs, and only narrowly missed crashing into Mrs Peabody, who just happened to be passing.

"Well, obviously all went well! I just thought I'd amble over…"

"In case I was murdered? Gran, they were scared witless I was going to tell on them. I enjoyed every minute. And Mac is coming with me, next Saturday afternoon, and then one day I'm going to take him on top of a double-decker bus, and another time it's going to be the Wildlife Park, if you and Mum will come too. I've got great plans for Mac!"

And Lizzie and her granny walked back to Barrow Lane with smiles on both their faces.

Bobbles and Baubles

One icy morning in early December Mrs Giles had a letter that wasn't a bill. Lizzie was trying to unjam her anorak zip, or she would already have left for school.

"Oh goodness glory! It's from Mr Bailey's daughter. You know, your new Auntie Sue. She's invited both of us *and* Mrs Peabody to spend Christmas with them!"

Lizzie forgot her zip, and bounced round the kitchen squealing with joy.

"They've organized a room for me and your gran, but would you mind having the top bunk in Tabitha's room? She's the little one, isn't she?"

"That would be gorgeous. Oh, what marvellous news for a rotten old Thursday!" and Lizzie dashed off to school to tell Lucy, her open anorak flying in the freezing fog.

When she came home, however, her mother was looking worried. "We can't possibly go. Think of all the extra presents! Ten pounds goes nowhere nowadays, and I wouldn't want to give them rubbish. Collecting relatives is expensive, Lizzie."

Lizzie looked stricken. Then determined.

"Mum, we'll make presents. All of them. That'll be cheaper."

"What on earth could we make? Neither of us is clever enough, and it's December already."

"I'll think of something," Lizzie promised.

"You'd better," her mum replied grimly.

At breakfast next morning Lizzie looked smug. "Bobble hats!" she exploded triumphantly. "One each, in different colours, so they'll know whose is whose. In very thick wool so they'll be quick to knit. I can make bobbles, I know how, and I could do the ribbing bit, if you could do the casting on and decreasing part. We'd only have to get one big ball of wool at a time, and sometimes you can get them on special offer. If we started today we'd get them all done in time."

So that was how the bobble hat factory began. They knitted like mad every evening – soft, tweedy colours for the grown-ups and bright ones for the girls. They made identical navy ones for the twins, but one had a red bobble and one had white. Possibly the nicest one of all was the last one they made, a little rainbow one from all the end bits of wool, with a jumbo bobble on top, for Mac. Lizzie planned to give it to him in the playground at the end of term.

Lizzie and her mum were expecting to find a fairly large Victorian house when they got off the bus at the roundabout on Christmas Eve, but when they actually stood outside it, the sheer size of the place made them gulp.

"It's the dark," Mum said nervously. "Things always look bigger in the dark."

"Wonder which bit Grandpa lives in," Lizzie said faintly.

Her hands felt damp inside her gloves as she groped for the bell. The door itself was the size of a church door and looked as if it hadn't been opened for weeks. A disembodied voice hit them from behind, and they both jumped. "Front door's jammed. It always sticks in winter. Come round to the back, it's what we always do."

A small figure emerged backwards from a huge clump of rhododendrons, shook itself like a little dog, whistled piercingly into the night air and trotted round the side of the house. An answering whistle came from somewhere in the garden.

"Davy or Jamie?" wondered Lizzie, stumbling a little as they followed the boy.

Grandpa welcomed them both at the back door, and took their coats and cases.

"Mildred's arrived already. Come along to the kitchen, everybody's there."

The kitchen was almost as large as the one at school, and the Aga cooker was the biggest Mrs Giles had ever seen. Meeting the family could have been a terrible ordeal for both of them, but Auntie Sue and Uncle Brian were friendlier than they had dared to hope. At first the five children stared at Lizzie and she felt very uncomfortable, but then a pan

started to boil over and Auntie Sue began yelling orders to get the table laid in double quick time, or nobody would be having any supper. Lizzie found herself clutching mats and handfuls of spoons and running with the others backwards and forwards between the kitchen and the dining room. It proved to be a marvellous way of breaking the ice.

"Sorry Mum's gone frantic," whispered Hannah, the tallest girl. "It's our fault really. We were supposed to do this earlier," and she began feverishly counting plates.

"We were trying to wrap Grandpa's present, only it was being awkward," hissed

the dark-haired one, Julia, grabbing a pile of forks and dropping half of them. "Watering cans are an impossible shape to wrap."

"It's because it's Christmas Eve," whispered one of the twins, almost colliding with her.

"She'll be OK after supper, you'll see," grunted the other one, blocking a doorway with an extra chair. "Grown-ups always get Blood Pressure on Christmas Eve. It's the waiting."

"You've got the top bunk in my room," Tabitha said, so quietly that Lizzie had to bend down to ask her to say it again. "It will be nice sharing my room with you. All the others share rooms except me, and I get lonely."

It was comforting to be treated as one of the family, instead of being made to feel like a visitor, Lizzie decided, and after supper she helped to make table decorations with the older girls, using tall white candles, red baubles and pieces of ivy. All the grown-ups were in the kitchen supposedly organizing the cooking for tomorrow, but it sounded more like a party as Mrs Peabody was introducing them to her vintage elderflower wine. Lizzie felt proud, because she had designed the labels for that batch.

All the children were sent to bed early that evening. As Lizzie climbed quietly into the top bunk above Tabitha, who was already asleep, and saw their two stockings dangling from the ladder, she felt fizzy all over with sheer happiness.

The twins woke them at quarter past five on Christmas Day.

"Bring your stocking and we'll go up to the girls' room and open them all together," one of the twins hissed into Lizzie's ear.

"But for goodness sake don't drop anything, or you'll wake Grandad. His Christmas spirit doesn't start for another three and a quarter hours," the other twin whispered.

"And last year he woke everybody up

shouting that it was *his* house after all, and if a poor old man couldn't get any sleep on Christmas morning, he'd turn us all out into the snow."

"Only it wasn't snowing. We still had to go back to bed though and Grandad said Father Christmas obviously didn't have grandchildren or he wouldn't have put cap guns in our stockings."

"Actually, I heard him say Father Christmas was a damn fool, but luckily Mum and Dad didn't hear it. He was all right by breakfast, though." They crept up the stairs, guarding their stockings with both arms, so they wouldn't bang the bannisters. "Bit early, isn't it?" Julia groaned as Davy and Jamie sat down on her bed.

"We thought we'd get this part over first so you could have a really long sleep afterwards," Jamie explained cunningly.

"All right. But no mouth-organs yet, and no fast-revving cars." So they munched nut-crunches and chocolate ladybirds, played

with miniature packs of cards and metal
puzzles, and had obstacle races over the
duvets with the joke hairy spiders. There had
been one in each stocking and you could
make the spiders jump by squeezing a rubber
bulb at the end of a thin plastic tube. When
everything had been eaten, the twins, Lizzie
and Tabitha were sent back to bed. They
went quickly and without any fuss.

"Before they start complaining about all
the crumbs and bits of silver paper we've left
in their beds," the twins giggled as they crept
downstairs.

* * *

"In this family," Grandpa announced at breakfast, some time later, "everyone who isn't cooking goes to church in the morning. Hannah, Julia and the twins are in the choir, so Lizzie, would you sit next to Tabitha and help her find the right words on her carol-sheet?"

"I'm allowed to sing 'la' if I don't know the words, but lots of them I do because of hearing the others practising," Tabitha said seriously. So they all trooped off to church, leaving Uncle Brian in charge of the dinner. It was all very cheerful, particularly when Jamie's joke spider fell out of his pocket as he was getting out his collection money. Mrs Peabody picked it up and put it in her bag, and Davie giggled.

The Christmas dinner looked like a banquet to Lizzie, and Auntie Sue said that her table decoration had put the finishing touch to it. Lizzie didn't really believe her, but it made her feel happy all the same.

Then Grandpa raised his glass: "Happy Christmas everybody, and specially to the three new members of our family. I'd like to propose a toast to adoptions in general and to our Lizzie in particular." Everybody clapped, and Lizzie went pink, but the twins surreptitiously pulled a cracker under the table, and made everyone jump as well as laugh, so Lizzie didn't feel embarrassed for long.

It was the biggest meal she had ever eaten, and the largest washing-up session she had ever helped with, then everybody gathered round the tree while Uncle Brian and Auntie Sue handed out presents to everyone.

Everyone except Lizzie, that is. The bobble hats were a great success and Gran and Grandpa insisted on wearing theirs. Tabitha used hers to put her smallest presents in for safe keeping. Soon the floor was knee-high in wrapping paper, and everyone's arms were full of presents. Except for Lizzie. She tried hard not to feel jealous as she saw the last tiny parcel being taken from the tree, and just when she felt she could bear it no longer, Grandpa said to the twins, "There's one left outside in the hallway. Must have been a special delivery. Bring it in, you two, only carefully mind, or I'll break your necks."

They staggered in carrying something large and heavy, wrapped in a jumbo-sized plastic Christmas sack. Everybody "ooh-ed" and "aah-ed" as they rushed to clear a space on the floor. Grandpa made an awful fuss about not being able to find the label, and *then* not having his glasses, and *then* not being able to read the writing. The suspense was dreadful. Finally, all in a rush, he read, "It says… 'For

my special extra granddaughter, with love from us all.' Must be for you, Lizzie. You haven't had any presents yet. Did you think we'd forgotten you, or are you always so patient?"

"Jammee dodger," said Davy. "It's bigger than everyone else's put together!"

Everybody watched while Lizzie unwrapped it. Then she gasped. It was the most beautiful wooden table-top desk, with a little brass lock and key and her initials *E.G.* painted on the sloping front.

"So that's what you were making in your workshop, when you wouldn't let us in!" Tabitha said accusingly.

"Oh, Grandpa," Lizzie breathed.

"Open it up, then," someone called out excitedly, and Lizzie unlocked the sloping lid. The inside was full of little drawers and compartments. And inside each one was a present for her from her five new cousins, from her auntie and uncle, and from her gran and Mum.

When she had finished unwrapping

everything, and thanking everybody in turn, Grandpa suggested that they had tea and Christmas cake. But he kept a restraining hand on Lizzie's shoulder. "One last thing," he said quietly, as the others trooped out, "you haven't discovered the secret place yet." He slid a small panel to one side to reveal a tiny secret space.

"Didn't want to show you in front of the others, or it wouldn't be a secret any more. It's for special things, Lizzie." Lizzie bent her head sideways to peep in and saw an envelope. Slowly she took it out and opened it. Out fell a photograph of Mac, laughing at her under a rainbow bobble hat. His nose was still running...

"Mildred took that the day before yesterday. She had an awful job getting a print in time. But you couldn't have one of your family missing at Christmas, could you?"

"It's perfect, Grandpa. And now we're all here! I'll never forget today, not even when I'm ancient."

"Well, let's get some tea, before all the wolves finish the cake."

As Lizzie followed her grandpa towards the kitchen she knew what she was going to hide in the secret compartment. It had to be her list! Once she had drawn in the final border decoration to finish it off, of course. Lizzie smiled to herself at the thought that there would be just enough room to squeeze in a pattern of dustbins and bobble hats.